THE FIRST DAY

by Nat Gabriel
illustrated by Eric Larsen

Scott Foresman

Editorial Offices: Glenview, Illinois • New York, New York
Sales Offices: Reading, Massachusetts • Duluth, Georgia
Glenview, Illinois • Carrollton, Texas • Menlo Park, California

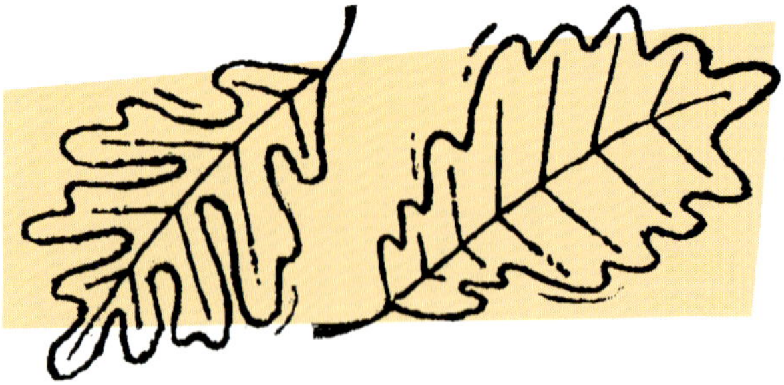

"How was your first day?" Katie's mother asked as she opened the apartment door.

"It was a disaster! My math class is in a converted broom closet, the halls are crowded, and there's not one normal person in the whole school. Other than that, it's wonderful," Katie said. Then she dropped her book bag on the floor and ran to her room.

Katie and her mother had made the big move to New York City just two weeks before school started. They left behind many good friends, happy memories, and a big house with several acres of land.

Katie's mom worked for a bank and they'd offered her a good job with much better pay if she would move. So they had packed up their belongings and moved to New York.

17 B

Katie leaped onto her bed and buried her face in the pillow. Her mother came in and patted her back for a minute before she spoke.

"Change is always difficult, Katie."

"I don't want things to change," Katie said. "I liked things the way they were. Who wants to live in the middle of all this concrete? They don't even have trees here. It's just not normal!"

"There are trees here—just not as many as we had in Michigan. New York City is a very exciting place to live, Katie."

"It's not exciting. It's horrible!" Katie sobbed into the pillow.

"Do you have homework due tomorrow?" asked Katie's mom. Katie shook her head.

"Do you have a list of supplies you need to buy for school?"

"Yes," said Katie as she dried her eyes with her shirt sleeve. "But the most important thing I need is new jeans."

"We just bought those jeans, Katie."

"Well, they're not the right kind. Nobody is wearing this kind and everyone stared at me today. It was awful."

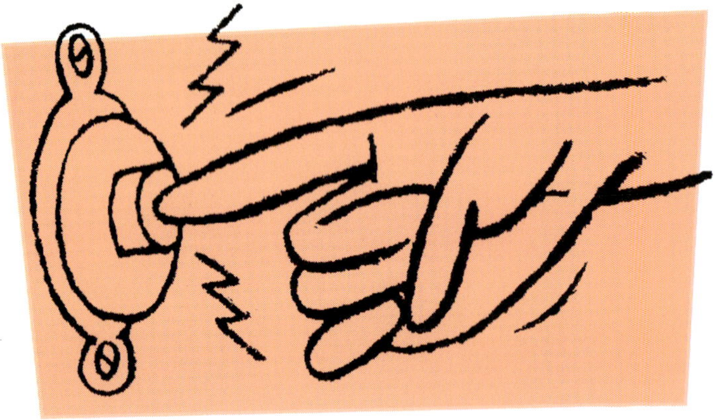

Just then the doorbell rang.

"I wonder who that is?" asked Katie's mom as she went to answer the door.

"Hi. I'm Emma. I'm in Katie's class. Is she home? Oh, I almost forgot, these are for you. My mom baked them."

Katie's mother smiled and took the plate of cookies. "Thanks. Come on in, Emma. Katie is in her room. I'll go get her."

Emma stood in the hall shifting from one foot to the other while she waited for Katie.

"Oh, hi," said Katie when she emerged and saw Emma standing in the hall. "How did you know where I live?"

"I live here too," said Emma.

"You do?" said Katie in amazement.

17B

Emma and Katie chatted for a while and then Emma asked Katie if she wanted to go downstairs and see her apartment.

"I live in 6-B. It's the same as your apartment except not as high up. The view is different."

"May I go, Mom?" asked Katie.

"Of course," her mother replied.

On the way down in the elevator, Katie asked Emma where she had bought her jeans.

"Oh, you can get these anywhere, but they're such a pain," said Emma as she pulled the pants up around her waist. "They fall down all the time, and you can't run in them or you trip. Your jeans make a lot more sense. Besides, no one else has jeans like yours, so they're sort of cool."

"Really?" asked Katie.

Emma nodded and smiled at Katie. Katie smiled back.

In Emma's apartment the two girls sat around talking about school and teachers. They ate the whole plate of cookies Emma's mother brought in to them.

"Where are you from, anyway?" asked Emma.

"Michigan," said Katie.

"What's Michigan like?" asked Emma.

"Well, it's pretty different from New York," answered Katie. "There are more trees, less concrete, and much less traffic. And as you may have noticed, people there have a different accent."

"Sounds nice, but how is the pizza? New York has great pizza, you know," said Emma as she broke the last cookie in half and handed half to Katie.

Later, Katie went back upstairs. Her mother was eager to hear about her new friend.

"I like Emma," said Katie. "She's nice."

"She seems like a very nice girl. Even if her pants are three sizes too big!" chuckled Katie's mother.

After dinner Katie and her mother went for a stroll. They walked down Broadway, one of the busiest streets in New York City. There was so much to look at.

They paused in front of a store window.

"Are those the jeans that you want?" inquired Katie's mom as she pointed at a pair of baggy pants.

"Actually, I decided I like the jeans I have, Mom. Nobody else is wearing this kind. So they're sort of special in a way."

Katie's mother smiled. "You're sort of special too!"

On the way home they stopped and bought hot pretzels from a cart on the corner. A man was sitting on a box on the sidewalk strumming a guitar. A crowd had gathered around him to listen. Katie and her mom stood and listened to him play while they munched on their pretzels.

"This is fun," said Katie as they walked back to their new home. "I see what you mean about New York being an exciting place to be. There's a lot going on."

TIPS

Later, Katie's mom came in to say good night.

"What started off as a bad day turned out to be a pretty good day in the end, didn't it?" she said as she leaned over and kissed Katie's cheek. "Things will get back to normal as soon as we settle in here."

"I still miss the trees, Mom," whispered Katie.

"I know. I do too, Katie."

"But I like the pretzels. And I like Emma too."

"I think you're going to find a lot of new things that you like here, Katie," said her mother as she turned out the light. "Sweet dreams."

"Hey, Mom? Let's get pizza for dinner tomorrow. I hear New York has great pizza."